Quarto is the authority on a wide range of topics.

Quarto educates, entertains and enriches the lives of
our readers—enthusiasts and lovers of hands-on living.

www.quartoknows.com

First published in the UK in 2017 by Frances Lincoln Children's Books,
an imprint of The Quarto Group, The Old Brewery, 6 Blundell Street London, N7 9BH
QuartoKnows.com
Visit our blogs at QuartoKids.com

Important: there are age restrictions for most blogging and social media sites and
in many countries parental consent is also required. Always ask permission from
your parents. Website information is correct at time of going to press. However, the
publishers cannot accept liability for any information or links found on any Internet
sites, including third-party websites.

A catalogue record for this book is available from the British Library.

ISBN 978-1-84780-871-4

Illustrated with mixed media
Designed by Karissa Santos
Edited by Katie Cotton
Published by Rachel Williams

Printed in China
1 3 5 7 9 8 6 4 2

FLUFFYWUFFY

Frances Lincoln
Children's Books

Mr Moot lived all alone
with his beloved pet Fluffywuffy.

Mr Moot was not
troubled by mice.

He did not have noisy
neighbours.

'I do like a nice, quiet life,' said Mr Moot.

And he hardly ever got
any letters delivered...

Then one day, there was a knock at the door.

'I've come for a week,' said Cousin Clarence,
'or a month, or quite possibly a year!'

'Oh dear!' said Mr Moot.
'I mean, come in and make
yourself at home. Meet Fluffywuffy!'

Cousin Clarence made himself at home immediately.

'I am very sleepy,' he declared, and he put himself
to bed on the living room sofa.

'I don't suppose he'll be much
bother,' said Mr Moot.

Fluffywuffy said nothing.

That night, Mr Moot was woken by a noise.

A noise of enormous proportions.

Whatever could it be?

Mr Moot switched on the living room light.
'Sometimes,' said Cousin Clarence,
'I just like a little night music.'

'Well, as long as it's
only sometimes,'
said Mr Moot, 'I expect
it won't be a bother.'

Fluffywuffy
said nothing.

The next night, Mr Moot was woken again, by another, quite different, but equally enormous noise. What could be happening now?

Mr Moot switched on the living room light.

'Sometimes,' said Cousin Clarence, 'I just get the urge to **make** something.'

'As long as it's only **sometimes**, I suppose it's okay,' said Mr Moot. 'And as long as you're **trying** not to be a bother.'
'I most certainly **am** trying,' said Cousin Clarence happily.

Fluffywuffy said nothing.

But the **next** night, well! Mr Moot was woken by another enormous **noise**.

A noise that was almost impossible to describe.

Mr Moot switched on the living room light.

'Friday nights only!' said Cousin Clarence
before Mr Moot could say a word.
'I find it very relaxing after a hard week.'

'Well **that's** all right then, I suppose,' said Mr Moot,
who was having a bit of a hard week himself.
'After all, **next** Friday **is** seven days away.'
Fluffywuffy said nothing.

Not very surprisingly, the **next** night,
Mr Moot could not get to sleep. He lay awake,
waiting for a **noise** to begin.

And after a while there
was a noise: a noise entirely
impossible to describe.

It was not the sound
of motorbikes...

or drums...

or circular
saws...

It was a noise
that got louder,
and louder
until suddenly—

SCRUNK!
(Perhaps the oddest noise
of all.) And then there was
complete and utter silence!

Mr Moot listened:
the silence
persisted.

He listened some more: the silence went on...
'Perhaps,' he said to himself in worried tones,
'I had better go and see.'

Mr Moot switched on the living room light and...

Cousin Clarence
was not there!

'Gone!' said Mr Moot. 'Disappeared!
Without so much as a goodbye or a thank you!'

Fluffywuffy said nothing.

'Mind you,' said Mr Moot,
'isn't it lovely and quiet?'
Fluffywuffy said nothing.

'Night night, Fluffywuffy!' said Mr Moot,
switching off the light. 'Sleep tight!'

And Fluffywuffy smiled...
but Fluffywuffy said nothing.